To Henry and Arlo,
my wonderfully imaginative little rascals.
—L.B.

For Marcie and Richard.
—W.K.

Book design by Melissa Nelson Greenberg

Library of Congress Cataloging-in-Publication Data available.
ISBN: 978-1-944903-12-1

Printed in China

10 9 8 7 6 5 4 3 2 1

Cameron Kids is an imprint of Cameron + Company

Cameron + Company
Petaluma, CA
www.cameronbooks.com

WALNUT ANIMAL SOCIETY

MAGNOLIA'S MAGNIFICENT MAP

by Lauren Bradshaw

Illustrated by Wednesday Kirwan

cameron kids

Deep in the shade of the walnut grove, the members of the *Walnut Animal Society* are busy preparing for a very special evening.

The Society Soirée comes just once a month, when the night is clear and the stars are bright.

Tonight, it is Magnolia the Bunny's turn to share her work.

Henry the Fox tests
his latest invention.

Chester the Raccoon
sets up chairs.

Ruthie the Deer
strings lights.

Margaux the Kitty writes an introduction for Magnolia's presentation.

And Eleanor the Bear bakes tea cakes.

Everyone is excited.

Everyone but Magnolia, that is.

It has taken her months of exploring and sketching and picture-snapping to create her latest map.

A map of the walnut grove.

There is just one problem. It isn't finished.

Magnolia's map is missing a spot.

"Magnolia?" Margaux called, as she walked in to check on her friend on the morning of the soirée. "What's the matter?" she asked.

"My map isn't finished!" Magnolia cried. "There's still one spot I haven't explored. I have to go!"

"I'll come with you!" Margaux said, grabbing her journal.

Together, the two friends scurried out into the walnut grove,
past the butterfly garden where Ruthie likes to dance,
through the meadow where Eleanor gathers flowers to make tea,
and past the patch where Henry's fireflies light up the night sky.

Finally, the two arrived at the last spot Magnolia had recorded on her map—the river mouth. Above them, a steep mountain loomed. The two friends looked at each other and then looked up.

Magnolia had to find out what was at the top.
But how would they ever get up there?

PLOP.

Magnolia and Margaux spun around at the sound of a fishing lure landing in the river. They squinted as they looked up to see where it had come from.

"Chester!" they cried in unison.

"What are you two up to?" Chester hollered.

"I need to finish my map," Magnolia said, "and the top of this mountain is my missing spot."

"How in the world did YOU get up there?" Margaux asked, ready to take note.

"It's easy," Chester shrugged as he landed in front of them with a thud. "Follow me."

It was not easy.

Magnolia and Margaux followed Chester's lead from wobbly rock to wobbly rock.

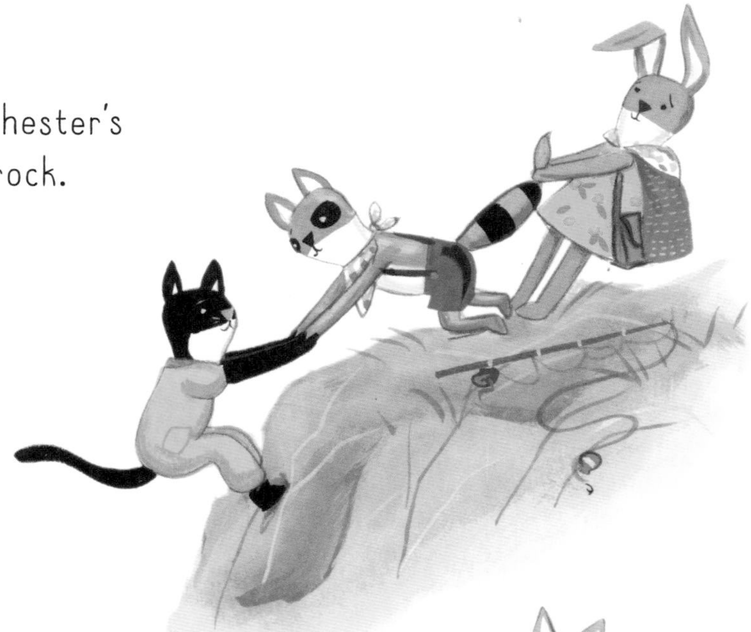

And up they went, higher and higher, pushing and pulling each other as best as they could.

Finally, on the tip-top of the mountain, Magnolia could see the entire walnut grove, every spot she'd ever explored.

And more.

"LOOK!" Margaux said.

Magnolia turned and saw what she had struggled so hard to find. At the top of the mountain was a glorious waterfall pouring into a perfect swimming hole.

"So this is where the water in the river comes from!" Chester cried.

This was the missing piece. Magnolia could hardly wait to add it.

But first, the three friends splashed in the waterfall and swam in the cool pool. Magnolia snapped pictures and Margaux took notes.

And then, Magnolia unrolled her map and added the missing spot. Her map was complete!

Just in time for tonight's event.

The Soirée!

It was time to go!

Back at the tree house, everyone took their seats.

Margaux introduced her friend.

And then Magnolia proudly unveiled her map.
It was magnificent.

Her friends' faces lit up as she pointed out each spot . . .

Ruthie's Butterfly Garden,
Eleanor's Tea Meadow, Henry's Firefly Patch,
Chester's Cove, Margaux's Waterfall.

"Where's your spot, Magnolia?" Eleanor asked.

"Magnolia's Mountain," she beamed,
"where I can see it all."

Walnut Grove
Ruthie's Butterfly Garden
Treehouse
INK
Chester's Cove

...nolia's Mountain
Eleanor's Tea Meadow
Margaux's Waterfall
Henry's Firefly Patch